THE TALE OF TWO NAUGHTIES

ISBN 978-1-63784-072-6 (paperback)
ISBN 978-1-63784-073-3 (digital)

Copyright © 2025 by T.W. Valentine

All rights reserved. No part of this publication may be reproduced, distributed, or transmitted in any form or by any means, including photocopying, recording, or other electronic or mechanical methods without the prior written permission of the publisher. For permission requests, solicit the publisher via the address below.

Hawes & Jenkins Publishing
16427 N Scottsdale Road Suite 410
Scottsdale, AZ 85254
www.hawesjenkins.com

Printed in the United States of America

THE TALE OF TWO NAUGHTIES

T.W. Valentine

Good evening, children!

I have a story to tell of two little naughties that didn't behave very well. They fussed, and they fought, argued, and talked back only to leave time-out, then go back! The two little naughties did not appreciate this and had much dismay because they were focused on having their own way.

Little did they know, it was for their own good that they needed to learn obedience and *that* they would.

In a home not too far away lived two little naughties that didn't obey. They misbehaved at school and disobeyed for fun. They never listened, and it started as the day begun.

Naughty One was to first to awaken because G. G. was in the kitchen making eggs and baking. G. G. loved both naughties very, very much, and she wanted them to stay in touch—in touch with the God of the universe and make Him happy. She had to teach them and make the lesson snappy! G. G. wanted them to learn how to obey, how to love God, to trust, and in His boundaries, to stay.

G. G. thought and prayed to God Almighty; she wanted to teach the naughties because disobedience is not to be taken lightly.

"Aha!" said G. G. as she laid her heart bare.

Because G. G. was obedient, God answered her prayer. A lesson for the naughties that they ne'er forget so that the love of obedience in their hearts would be set!

Naughty One bounced into the kitchen. And what did she see? G. G. smiling toward God as big as can be!

Naughty One said, "Good morning, my G. G. Now I'm awake, I'm ready to eat. Can you bake a cake?"

"Good morning, Little One!" G. G. replied. "I have made you breakfast, but your request for cake has been denied. First you must wash up and prepare for this day, brush your teeth, wash your face, brush your hair, and not play. That comes later… Wait, did you pray? Did you thank God Almighty for awakening you to another glorious day?"

Naughty One replied, "No, I did not. I don't know what to say. I just woke up, and I'm ready to play!"

G. G. was shocked and, with her left eyebrow raised, said very firmly to this naughty one, "Listen, Little One, I want to be clear. This day is not about you, my dear! You slept sound and safe all through the night. You woke up healthy and happy without a fright. Even if things are not as perfect as planned, we are to thank our wonderful God because He is God, and we are man. Now off to your tasks as you have been told, but those prayers must come first as they are due. Oh yes, where is Little Two?"

"Little Two is still in bed. Little Two is acting like a sleepyhead. Are you going to make Little Two brush teeth and comb hair? Are you going—"

With a quick reply and an abrupt turn, G. G. responded with a stern, "No sass! No talking back! We won't have any of that! You are to be concerned only with your tasks to be done because talking back are actions of a naughty one. Now happy face and do not pout because it is much too early for time out!" G. G. smiled and, with a kiss on the head, sent Little One to get Little Two out of bed.

Upon entering their bedroom, what did Little One see? Little Two with brushed teeth and combed hair, smiling as big as can be!

"Good morning," said Little Two to Little One. "How about this morning we have lots of fun? We can dress up for school in our favorite costume! I'll wear my cowboy hat, and since we don't have a real horse, I'll take the broom!"

Little One laughed and hooted and agreed with a smile.

Little One decided to be a superhero with style. So off to the bathroom to brush teeth and comb hair… But wait! What about what G. G. said about prayer?

Little One paused to stop and think, then Little Two came down the hall on the broom and said, "The last one to the breakfast table is a stink!"

So in a hurry, Little One began the task of morning care, brushing teeth and combing hair.

After Little One finished the morning routine, Little One rushed to the breakfast table happy and with a glowing beam! Little One decided to be a superhero of blue—blue pants, blue shirt, blue hat, and even blue boots that were made for combat!

As G. G. served breakfast to the naughties, she was absolutely startled!

At the two little naughties, she stared and marveled. "Where on earth do you imagine yourselves to be attending school this day? Do you plan on going to school only to play?"

"G. G., we want to surprise our friends at school by wearing this disguise. We will dress up in costume. We will have fun. We will laugh and play until the day is done!" exclaimed Little Two.

"Oh no! No! No! That is not what you will do! You will not surprise, you will not wear a costume. This day is not about your fun. This day is not your day. This day has tasks to be done! This is time for school, time for learning, time to work, time for earning! Right now is time to be dressed properly! Now off to your room and in your school uniform you will dress, and if you do not, discipline will serve you best!"

The two naughties gasped at the thought of discipline and started to cry.

Then in a firm voice, G. G. said, "No! Keep a dry eye! You two know better than to wake and play. Dressing improperly and wasting precious time at the beginning of the day…this is what happens when you do not pray! Now back to your room, all of us will go. To get dressed properly, to God with prayer our thanks we will show."

Reluctantly, the naughties returned to their rooms, and Naughty Two relinquished the broom. First on bended knee, each of them prayed, thanking God and asking for guidance throughout the day. Proper hair, proper clothes, and yummy breakfast, they ate.

Naughty One and Naughty Two were up on their feet, running to school, so they would not be late. They had prayed and were focused on a path that was straight.

About lunchtime came, a miracle. Naughty One and Naughty Two had scored happy faces on the behavior chart blackboard.

So happy and grateful to be able to obey, a sweet prayer Naughty Two did say. "Dear God, thank You that I can obey. Thank You that when I do, out of trouble I stay! I'm happy and can still go play! Amen! In Jesus's name, I pray!"

At the end of the day, when the final bell rang, a first-time victory, the two littles sang, "We did it! We did it! We did it! We obeyed! We listened, and out of trouble we stayed! We learned and listened, and in the boundaries, we stayed!"

Little Two sang, "Yes, yes, in the boundaries we did stay. I have an idea. We should do this every day! We can listen and we can pray!"

The moral of this story is, with prayer and correction, we can all find God's holy direction. As for the littles and G. G.'s prayer, God answered because of His love and care.

G. G. smiled, and she thanked God that the littles could no longer be called the naughties but now the little goods!

ABOUT THE AUTHOR

T.W. Valentine is a busy mom with a growing family in Nashville, TN. She loves writing and making indispensable life lessons relatable to children everywhere. Her stories are full of imagination, laughter and fun to enlighten children for the bright futures ahead of them.

www.ingramcontent.com/pod-product-compliance
Lightning Source LLC
LaVergne TN
LVHW070055060126
829164LV00056B/1976